Gymnastics

by Wil Mara

Content Consultant
Thomas Sawyer, EdD
Professor of Recreation and Sports Management
Indiana State University
Terre Haute, Indiana

Reading Consultant
Jeanne Clidas
Reading Specialist

Children's Press®
An Imprint of Scholastic Inc.
New York Toronto London Auckland Sydney
Mexico City New Delhi Hong Kong
Danbury, Connecticut

Library of Congress Cataloging-in-Publication Data
Mara, Wil.
  Gymnastics/by Wil Mara.
    p. cm.—(Rookie read-about sports)
  Includes bibliographical references and index.
  ISBN-13: 978-0-531-20859-5 (lib. bdg.)   ISBN-10: 0-531-20859-1 (lib. bdg.)
  ISBN-13: 978-0-531-20928-8 (pbk.)   ISBN-10: 0-531-20928-8 (pbk.)
  1. Gymnastics—Juvenile literature. I. Title. II. Series.
  GV461.3.M323 2012
  796.44—dc23   2011031372

1 2 3 4 5 6 7 8 9 10 R 21 20 19 18 17 16 15 14 13 12

Photographs © 2012: Alamy Images: 26 (Gabe Palmer), 16 (Image Source), 24, 31 top
right (Ted Foxx); Corbis Images: 6 top (Michael Mahovlich), 4 (Robert Glenn/DK Stock),
12, 28 (Ray Moller/Dorling Kindersley); iStockphoto: 8 (Tammy Bryngelson), 20,
31 bottom left (Алексей Многосмыслов); Media Bakery: 2, 28 handstands, 29
handstands, 30 handstands (Colleen Cahill), cover (Herb Watson), 14, 31 top
left (Thomas Barwick); Shutterstock, Inc.: 18, 19, 22, 31 bottom right (Jiang
Dao Hua), 6 bottom (Len44ik), 10 (Renata Osinska).

Table of Contents

Get Ready to Do Gymnastics

Gymnastics is a fun sport! You use your body in many ways.

You should always stretch first. This gets your body ready.

On the Mat

You use a large mat. The mat is soft.

10

You can roll forward like a ball. This move is called a forward roll.

12

You use both your hands
and feet to do a cartwheel.
Your body turns around like
a wheel.

Using the Balance Beam

The balance beam is long and thin. Using it takes practice.

You put one foot in front of the other. You must be very careful not to fall.

When You Are Older

You will get better the more you practice. You will do amazing moves as you get older.

Some boys use the rings.
Your arms must be very
strong to use the rings. You
have to pull your body up
and hold it there.

A girl swings on the uneven bars. These are two long bars. One bar is taller than the other.

The parallel bars also have two bars. One is just as high as the other. A gymnast swings between them.

Gymnastics is fun!
Gymnasts need good
balance so they don't fall.
They need to be strong to
do the moves.

Good Sportsmanship

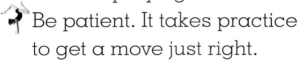 Respect yourself, the other kids, and the adults helping out.

Stay positive. Learn from your mistakes. And keep trying!

Be patient. It takes practice to get a move just right.

For . . .

Staying Fit

Eat right.

- Choose lots of fruits and vegetables.
- Eat 5 servings of grains. Whole wheat bread is good. So is oatmeal.
- Protein keeps you strong. Meat, eggs, and fish give you protein.
- Dairy makes strong bones. Milk and cheese are dairy.

Get plenty of sleep.

Practice gymnastics as much as you can.

Gymnastics Fun Facts

 Only women do rhythmic gymnastics. They do moves on the floor with ribbons, balls, and hoops.

 The person who won the most Olympic medals ever was a gymnast. Larissa Latynina won 18 medals.

Visit this Scholastic web site for more information on gymnastics: **www.factsfornow.scholastic.com**

Words You Know

balance beam

parallel bars

rings

uneven bars

Index

About the Author

Wil Mara is the award-winning author of more than 100 books, many of them educational titles for young readers. More information about his work can be found at *www.wilmara.com*.